The Tale of Fatty Coon

Arthur Scott Bailey

Copyright © 2023 Culturea Editions
Text and cover : © public domain
Edition : Culturea (Hérault, 34)
Contact : infos@culturea.fr
Print in Germany by Books on Demand
Design and layout : Derek Murphy
Layout : Reedsy (https://reedsy.com/)
ISBN : 9791041952861
Légal deposit : September 2023
All rights reserved

The Tale of Fatty Coon

I

FATTY COON AT HOME

Fatty Coon was so fat and round that he looked like a ball of fur, with a plumelike tail for a handle. But if you looked at him closely you would have seen a pair of very bright eyes watching you.

Fatty loved to eat. Yes—he loved eating better than anything else in the world. That was what made him so fat. And that, too, was what led him into many adventures.

Close by a swamp, which lay down in the valley, between Blue Mountain and Swift River, Fatty Coon lived with his mother and his brother and his two sisters. Among them all there was what grown people call "a strong family resemblance," which is the same thing as saying that they all looked very much alike. The tail of each one of them—mother and children too—had six black rings around it. Each of them had a dark brown patch of fur across the face, like a mask. And—what do you think?—each of them, even Fatty and his brother and his sisters, had a stiff, white moustache!

Of course, though they all looked so much alike, you would have known which was Mrs. Coon, for she was so much bigger than her children. And you would have known which was Fatty—he was so much rounder than his brother and his sisters.

Mrs. Coon's home was in the hollow branch of an old tree. It was a giant of a tree—a poplar close by a brook which ran into the swamp—and the branch which was Mrs. Coon's home was as big as most tree-trunks are.

Blackie was Fatty's brother—for the mask on his face was just a little darker than the others'. Fluffy was one of Fatty's sisters, because her fur was just a little fluffier than the other children's. And Cutey was the other sister's name, because she was so quaint.

Now, Fatty Coon was forever looking around for something to eat. He was never satisfied with what his mother brought home for him. No matter how big a dinner Mrs. Coon set before her family, as soon as he had finished eating his share Fatty would wipe his white moustache carefully — for all the world like some old gentleman—and hurry off in search of something more.

Sometimes he went to the edge of the brook and tried to catch fish by hooking them out of the water with his sharp claws. Sometimes he went over to the swamp and hunted for duck among the tall reeds. And though he did not yet know how to catch a duck, he could always capture a frog or two; and Fatty ate them as if he hadn't had a mouthful of food for days.

To tell the truth, Fatty would eat almost anything he could get—nuts, cherries, wild grapes, blackberries, bugs, small snakes, fish, chickens, honey—there was no end to the different kinds of food he liked. He ate everything. And he always wanted more.

"Is this all there is?" Fatty Coon asked his mother one day. He had gobbled up every bit of the nice fish that Mrs. Coon had brought home for him. It was gone in no time at all.

Mrs. Coon sighed. She had heard that question so many times; and she wished that for once Fatty might have all the dinner he wanted.

"Yes—that's all," she said, "and I should think that it was enough for a young coon like you."

Fatty said nothing more. He wiped his moustache on the back of his hand (I hope you'll never do that!) and without another word he started off to see what he could find to eat.

II

FATTY LEARNS SOMETHING ABOUT EGGS

When Fatty Coon started off alone to find something more to eat, after finishing the fish that his mother had brought home for him, he did not know that he was going to have an adventure. He nosed about among the bushes and the tall grasses and caught a few bugs and a frog or two. But he didn't think that THAT was much. He didn't seem to have much luck, down on the ground. So he climbed a tall hemlock, to see if he could find a squirrel's nest, or some bird's eggs.

Fatty loved to climb trees. Up in the big hemlock he forgot, for a time, that he was still hungry. It was delightful to feel the branches swaying under him, and the bright sunshine was warm upon his back. He climbed almost to the very tip-top of the tree and wound himself around the straight stem. The thick, springy branches held him safely, and soon Fatty was fast asleep. Next to eating, Fatty loved sleeping. And now he had a good nap.

Fatty Coon woke up at last, yawned, and slowly unwound himself from the stem of the tree. He was terribly hungry now. And he felt that he simply MUST find something to eat at once.

Without going down to the ground, Fatty climbed over into the top of another big tree and his little beady, bright eyes began searching all the branches carefully. Pretty soon Fatty smiled. He smiled because he was pleased. And he was pleased because he saw exactly what he had been looking for. Not far below him was a big nest, built of sticks and lined with bark and moss. It was a crow's nest, Fatty decided, and he lost no time in slipping down to the crotch of the tree where the nest was perched.

There were four white eggs in the nest—the biggest crow's eggs Fatty had ever seen. And he began to eat them hungrily. His nose became smeared with egg, but he didn't mind that at all. He kept thinking how good the eggs tasted—and how he wished there were more of them.

There was a sudden rush through the branches of the tall tree. And Fatty Coon caught a hard blow on his head. He felt something sharp sink into his back, too. And he clutched at the edge of the nest to keep from falling.

Fatty was surprised, to say the least, for he had never known crows to fight like that. And he was frightened, because his back hurt. He couldn't fight, because he was afraid he would fall if he let go of the nest.

There was nothing to do but run home as fast as he could. Fatty tried to hurry; but there was that bird, beating and clawing his back, and pulling him first one way and then another. He began to think he would never reach home. But at last he came to the old poplar where his mother lived. And soon, to his great joy, he reached the hole in the big branch; and you may well believe that Fatty was glad to slip down into the darkness where his mother, and his brother Blackie, and Fluffy and Cutey his sisters, were all fast asleep. He was glad, because he knew that no crow could follow him down there.

Mrs. Coon waked up. She saw that Fatty's back was sadly torn (for coons, you know, can see in the dark just as well as you can see in the daylight).

"What on earth is the matter?" she exclaimed.

Poor Fatty told her. He cried a little, because his back hurt him, and because he was so glad to be safe at home once more.

"What color were those eggs?" Mrs. Coon inquired.

"White!" said Fatty.

"Ah, ha!" Mrs. Coon said. "Don't you remember that crows' eggs are a blueish green? That must have been a goshawk's nest. And a goshawk is the fiercest of all the hawks there are. It's no wonder your back is clawed. Come here and let me look at it."

Fatty Coon felt quite proud, as his mother examined the marks of the goshawk's cruel claws. And he didn't feel half as sorry for himself as you might think, for he remembered how good the eggs had tasted. He only wished there had been a dozen of them.

III

FATTY DISCOVERS MRS. TURTLE'S SECRET

After his adventure with the goshawk Fatty Coon did not go near the tree-tops for a long time. Whenever he left home he would crawl down the old poplar tree in which he lived; and he wouldn't climb a single tree until he came home again. Somehow, he felt safer on the ground. You see, he hadn't forgotten the fright he had had, nor how the goshawk's claws had hurt his back.

It was just three days after his scare, to be exact, when Fatty Coon found himself on the bank of the creek which flowed slowly into Swift River. Fatty had been looking for frogs, but he had had no luck at all. To tell the truth, Fatty was a little too young to catch frogs easily, even when he found one; and he was a good deal too fat, for he was so plump that he was not very spry.

Now, Fatty was hiding behind some tall rushes, and his sharp little eyes were looking all about him, and his nose was twitching as he sniffed the air. He wished he might find a frog. But not one frog appeared. Fatty began to think that some other coon must have visited the creek just before him and caught them all. And then he forgot all about frogs.

Yes! Frogs passed completely out of Fatty Coon's mind. For whom should he spy but Mrs. Turtle! He saw her little black head first, bobbing along through the water of the creek. She was swimming toward the bank where Fatty was hidden. And pretty soon she pulled herself out of the water and waddled a short distance along the sand at the edge of the creek.

Mrs. Turtle stopped then; and for a few minutes she was very busy about something. First she dug a hole in the sand. And Fatty wondered what she was looking for. But he kept very quiet. And after a time Mrs. Turtle splashed into the creek again and paddled away. But before she left she scooped sand into the hole she had dug. Before she left the place she looked all around, as if to make sure that no one had seen her. And as she waddled slowly to the water Fatty could see that she was smiling as if she was very well pleased about something. She seemed to have a secret.

Fatty Coon had grown very curious, as he watched Mrs. Turtle. And just as soon as she was out of sight he came out from his hiding place in the tall reeds and trotted down to the edge of the creek. He went straight to the spot where Mrs. Turtle had dug the hole and filled it up again. And Fatty was so eager to know what she had been doing that he began to dig in the very spot where Mrs. Turtle had dug before him.

It took Fatty Coon only about six seconds to discover Mrs. Turtle's secret. For he did not have to paw away much of the sand before he came upon — what do you suppose? Eggs! Turtles' eggs! Twenty-seven round, white eggs, which Mrs. Turtle had left there in the warm sand to hatch. THAT was why she looked all around to make sure that no one saw her. THAT was why she seemed so pleased. For Mrs. Turtle fully expected that after a time twenty-seven little turtles would hatch from those eggs — just as chickens do — and dig their way out of the sand.

But it never happened that way at all. For as soon as he got over his surprise at seeing them, Fatty Coon began at once to eat those twenty-seven eggs. They were delicious. And as he finished the last one he couldn't help thinking how lucky he had been.

IV

FATTY COON'S MISTAKE

Fatty Coon was very fond of squirrels. And you may think it strange when I tell you that not one of the squirrels anywhere around Blue Mountain was the least bit fond of Fatty Coon. But when I say that Fatty Coon was fond of squirrels, I mean that he liked to eat them. So of course you will understand now why the squirrels did not care for Fatty at all. In fact, they usually kept just as far away from him as they could.

It was easy, in the daytime, for the squirrels to keep out of Fatty's way, when he wandered through the tree-tops, for the squirrels were much sprier than Fatty. But at night—ah! that was a very different matter. For Fatty Coon's eyes were even sharper in the dark than they were in the daylight; but the poor squirrels were just as blind as you are when you are safely tucked in bed and the light is put out.

Yes—when the squirrels were in bed at night, up in their nests in the trees, they could see very little. And you couldn't say they were SAFE in bed, because they never knew when Fatty Coon, or his mother, or his brother, or one of his sisters, or some cousin of his, might come along and catch them before they knew it.

Fatty thought it great sport to hunt squirrels at night. Whenever he tried it he usually managed to get a good meal. And after he had almost forgotten about the fright the goshawk had given him in the tall hemlock he began to roam through the tree-tops every night in search of squirrels and sleeping birds.

But a night came at last when Fatty was well punished for hunting squirrels. He had climbed half-way to the top of a big chestnut tree, when he spied a hole in the trunk. He rather thought that some squirrels lived inside that hole. And as he listened for a few seconds he could hear something moving about inside. Yes! Fatty was sure that there was a squirrel in there—probably several squirrels.

Fatty Coon's eyes turned green. It was a way they had, whenever he was about to eat anything, or whenever he played with his brother Blackie, or Fluffy and Cutey, his sisters; or whenever he was frightened. And now Fatty was so sure that he was going to have a fine lunch that his eyes turned as green as a cat's. He reached a paw inside the hole and felt all around.

WOW! Fatty gave a cry; and he pulled his paw out much faster than he had put it in. Something had given him a cruel dig. And in a jiffy Fatty saw what that "something" was. It was a grumpy old tramp coon, whom Fatty had never seen before.

"What do you mean, you young rascal, by disturbing me like this?" the ragged stranger cried.

"Please, sir, I never knew it was you," Fatty stammered.

"Never knew it was me! Who did you think it was?"

"A—a squirrel!" Fatty said faintly. And he whimpered a little, because his paw hurt him.

"Ho, ho! That's a good one! That's a good joke!" The tramp coon laughed heartily. And then he scowled so fiercely that poor Fatty nearly tumbled out of the tree. "You go home," he said to Fatty. "And don't you let me catch you around here again. You hear?"

"Yes, sir!" Fatty said. And home he went. And you may be sure that he let THAT tree alone after that. He never went near it again.

V

FATTY COON GOES FISHING

One day Fatty Coon was strolling along the brook which flowed not far from his home. He stopped now and then, to crouch close to the water's edge, in the hope of catching a fish. And one time, when he lay quite still among the rocks, at the side of a deep pool, with his eyes searching the clear water, Fatty Coon suddenly saw something bright, all yellow and red, that lighted on the water right before him. It was a bug, or a huge fly. And Fatty was very fond of bugs—to eat, you know. So he lost no time. The bright thing had scarcely settled on the water when Fatty reached out and seized it. He put it into his mouth, when the strangest thing happened. Fatty felt himself pulled right over into the water.

He was surprised, for he never knew a bug or a fly to be so strong as that. Something pricked his cheek and Fatty thought that the bright thing had stung him. He tried to take it out of his mouth, and he was surprised again. Whatever the thing was, it seemed to be stuck fast in his mouth. And all the time Fatty was being dragged along through the water. He began to be frightened. And for the first time he noticed that there was a slender line which stretched from his mouth straight across the pool. As he looked along the line Fatty saw a man at the other end of it—a man, standing on the other side of the brook! And he was pulling Fatty toward him as fast as he could.

Do you wonder that Fatty Coon was frightened? He jumped back—as well as he could, in the water—and tried to swim away. His mouth hurt; but he plunged and pulled just the same, and jerked his head and squirmed and wriggled and twisted. And just as Fatty had almost given up hope of getting free, the gay-colored bug, or fly, or whatever it was, flew out of his mouth and took the line with it. At least, that was what Fatty Coon thought. And he swam quickly to the bank and scampered into the bushes.

Now, this was what really happened. Farmer Green had come up the brook to catch trout. On the end of his fish-line he had tied a make-believe fly, with a hook hidden under its red and yellow wings. He had stolen along the brook very quietly, so that he wouldn't frighten the fish. And he had made so little noise that Fatty Coon never heard him at all. Farmer Green had not seen Fatty, crouched as he was among the stones. And when Fatty reached out and grabbed the make-believe fly Farmer Green was even more surprised at what happened than Fatty himself. If the fish-hook hadn't worked loose from Fatty's mouth Farmer Green would have caught the queerest fish anybody ever caught, almost.

Something seemed to amuse Farmer Green, as he watched Fatty dive into the bushes; and he laughed loud and long. But Fatty Coon didn't laugh at all. His mouth was too sore; and he was too frightened. But he was very, very glad that the strange bug had flown away.

VI

FATTY AND THE GREEN CORN

It was mid-summer when Fatty Coon had what he then believed to be the finest time in all his life. And later, when he was older, he still thought that nothing had ever happened to him that was quite so enjoyable as that surprise his mother gave him when he was a young coon.

Of course it was something to eat—the surprise. You must have guessed that, knowing Fatty Coon as you do.

"Come, children!" Mrs. Coon said. "Come with me! I'm going to give you a treat—something specially nice."

"Is it something to eat?" Fatty asked, as they started off in the direction of Farmer Green's fields.

"Yes—and the best thing you ever tasted," Mrs. Coon said.

Fatty was greatly excited. His little bright eyes turned green in the moonlight. He wondered what the surprise would be. And, as usual, he was very hungry. He walked close beside his mother, for he wanted to be the first to taste the surprise. You would think that he would have wanted his two sisters to taste it first, and his brother Blackie, too. But you must not forget that Fatty was greedy. And greedy people are not thoughtful of others.

When Mrs. Coon turned out of the lane and crawled through the fence,

Fatty squeezed between the rails very nimbly, for him.

"Here we are!" said his mother.

Fatty looked about him. They stood in a field grown high with tall stalks of some sort, which turned to green, ribbon-like leaves half way up from the ground. Fatty grunted. He was very impolite, you see.

"Well—what is there to eat that's so fine?" he asked. "This stuff isn't good. It's like eating reeds." He had already bitten into one of the stalks.

"What do you call that?" Mrs. Coon asked. She showed Fatty a long roll of green that grew out of one of the stalks.

"That's something like a cattail," said Fatty. "It isn't good to eat."

"Have you ever tried one?" asked his mother.

"N—no," Patty said. "But Freddie Bluejay told me they weren't good."

"He did, did he?" Mrs. Coon said nothing more. She stood up on her hind legs and pulled one of the tall stalks down until she could reach that long, green thing that grew there. In a jiffy she had torn it from its stalk. And then she stripped the green covering off it. "Try that!" said Mrs. Coon with a smile.

Of course it was Fatty who tasted it first. He took a good mouthful of the white kernels, and he was overjoyed. Such sweetness! Such delicious, milky juice! It was a moment that Fatty never forgot.

Fatty began tearing down the stalks for himself and he never said another word until at last he simply had to stop eating just to catch his breath.

"What's its name, Mother?" he inquired.

"Corn, my child."

"Well, why doesn't Freddie Bluejay like it?" Fatty asked.

"He's probably very fond of corn," said Mrs. Coon. "And I've no doubt he was afraid that you would eat up this whole field, once you started."

"I'd like to," said Fatty, with a sigh. "I'd like to eat all the corn in the world."

<h1 style="text-align:center">VII</h1>

JOHNNIE GREEN IS DISAPPOINTED

It made Fatty Coon feel sad, just to think that there was that field full of corn, and that he could never eat all of it. But Fatty made up his mind that he would do the best he could. He would visit the cornfield every night and feast on those sweet, tender kernels.

The very next night Fatty set out toward Farmer Green's. It was hardly dark. But Fatty could not wait any longer. He could not even wait for his mother and his sisters and his brother. He hurried away alone. And when he came in sight of the cornfield he felt better. He had been the least bit afraid that the corn might be gone. He thought that maybe Farmer Green had picked it, or that some of the forest people had eaten it all. But there it was—a forest of corn, waving and rustling in the moonlight as the breeze touched it. Fatty felt very happy as he slipped through the rail-fence.

I wouldn't dare say how many ears of corn Fatty ate that night. And he would have eaten more, too, if it hadn't been for just one thing. A dog barked. And that spoiled Fatty's fun. For the dog was altogether too near for Fatty to feel safe. He even dropped the ear of corn he was gnawing and hurried toward the woods.

It was lucky for Fatty that he started when he did. For that dog was close behind him in no time. There was only one thing to do: Fatty knew that he must climb a tree at once. So he made for the nearest tree in sight—a big, spreading oak, which stood all alone just beyond the fence. And as Fatty crouched on a limb he felt safe enough, though the dog barked and whined, and leaped against the tree, and made a great fuss.

Fatty looked down at the dog and scolded a little. He was not afraid. But it made him cross to be driven out of the cornfield. And he wished the dog would go away. But the dog—it was Farmer Green's Spot—the dog had no idea of leaving. He stayed right there and barked so loudly that it was not

14

long before Farmer Green and his hired man came in sight. And with them was Johnnie Green and a little, young dog that had just been given to him.

When Farmer Green saw Fatty he seemed disappointed. "He's too young to bother with," he said. "His skin's not worth much. We'll go 'long and see what we can find."

But Johnnie Green stayed behind. He wanted that young coon. And he intended to have him, too. Leaving the young dog to watch Fatty Coon, Johnnie went back to the farmhouse. After a while he appeared again with an axe over his shoulder. And when he began to chop away at the big oak, Fatty Coon felt very uneasy. Whenever Johnnie drove his axe into the tree, both the tree and Fatty shivered together. And Fatty began to wish he had stayed away from the cornfield. But not for long, because Johnnie Green soon gave up the idea of chopping down the big oak. The wood was so hard to cut, and the tree was so big, that Johnnie had not chopped long before he saw that it would take him all night to cut through it. He looked up longingly at Fatty Coon. And Johnnie started to climb the tree himself. But the higher he climbed, the higher Fatty climbed. And Johnnie knew that he could never catch that plump young coon in that way.

At last Johnnie Green started off, calling his dog after him. And then Fatty Coon came down. But he did not go back to the cornfield. He decided that he had had adventures enough for one night. But Fatty had learned something—at least he thought he had. For he made up his mind that once he climbed a tree, no man could reach him. TREES COULD NOT BE CHOPPED DOWN! That was what Fatty believed. Perhaps you will know, later, whether Fatty ever found out that he was mistaken.

VIII

A TERRIBLE FRIGHT

It was the very next night after old dog Spot had treed Fatty Coon in the big oak near the cornfield. They had finished their evening meal at Farmer Green's house. The cows were milked, the horses had been fed, the chickens had all gone to roost. And Farmer Green looked up at the moon, rising from behind Blue Mountain.

"We'll go coon-hunting again to-night," he said to Johnnie and the hired man. "The corn has brought the coons up from the swamp. We'll start as soon as it grows a little darker."

Well—after a while they set out for the cornfield. And sure enough! old

Spot soon began to bark.

"He's treed!" said Farmer Green, pretty soon. And they all hurried over to the edge of the woods, where Spot had chased a coon up into a tall chestnut tree. In the moonlight they could see the coon quite plainly. "Another little feller!" cried Farmer Green. "I declare, all the coons that come to the cornfield seem to be young ones. This one's no bigger than the one we saw last night."

Now, although Farmer Green never guessed it, it was Fatty Coon who was up there in the tall chestnut. He had run almost to the woods this time, before he had to take to a tree. In fact, if Spot hadn't been quite so close to him Fatty could have reached the woods, and then he would have just jumped from one tree to another. But there were no trees near enough the big chestnut for that. Fatty had to stay right there and wait for those men to pass on. He wasn't afraid. He felt perfectly safe in his big tree. And he only smiled when Johnnie Green said to his father—

"I wish I had that young coon. He'd make a fine pet."

"A pet!" exclaimed Farmer Green. "You remember that pet fox you had, that stole my chickens?"

"Oh, I'd be careful," Johnnie promised. "Besides, don't you think we ought to catch him, so he won't eat any more corn?"

Farmer Green smiled. He had been a boy himself, once upon a time, and he had not forgotten the pet coon that he had owned when he was just about Johnnie's age.

"All right!" he said at last. "I'll give you one more chance, Johnnie. But you'll have to see that this young coon doesn't kill any of my poultry."

Johnnie promised that nothing of the sort should happen. And then his father and the hired man picked up their axes; and standing on opposite sides of the tall chestnut tree, they began to chop.

How the chips did fly! At the very first blow Fatty knew that this was an entirely different sort of chopping from that which Johnnie had attempted the night before. The great tree shook as if it knew that it would soon come crashing down upon the ground.

And as for Fatty Coon, he could not see but that he must fall when the tree did. He, too, shivered and shook. And he wrapped himself all the way around a limb and hung on as tight as ever he could.

IX

JOHNNIE GREEN LOSES HIS PET

Now, Farmer Green and his hired man had not chopped long before they stopped to breathe. They had not chopped long—but oh! what great, yawning holes they had made in the big chestnut! From the limb where he clung Fatty Coon looked down. The tree no longer shook. And Fatty felt better at once. You see, he thought that the men would go away, just as Johnnie had gone away the night before. But they had no such idea at all.

"Which way are you going to fell her?" the hired man asked. He said HER, meaning the TREE, of course.

"That way!" said Farmer Green, pointing toward the woods. "We'll have to drop her that way, or she'll fall right across the road, and of course THAT would never do."

"But will she clear the trees on the edge of the woods?" The hired man appeared somewhat doubtful.

"Oh, to be sure—to be sure!" answered Farmer Green.

And with that they set to work again. But this time they both chopped on the same side of the tree—the side toward the woods.

Now, if Fatty Coon was frightened before, you will believe that he was still more frightened when the big chestnut tree began to sag. Yes! it began to lean toward the woods. Slowly, slowly it tipped. And Fatty was scared half out of his mind. He climbed to the very top of the tree, because he wanted to get just as far away from those men as he could. And there he waited. There was nothing else he could do. Yes! he waited until that awful moment should come when the tree would go crashing down upon the ground. What was going to happen to him then? Fatty wondered. And while he was wondering there sounded all at once a great snapping and splitting. And Fatty felt the tree falling, falling. He could hear Johnnie Green shouting. And he shut his eyes and held fast to his branch. Then came the crash.

When Fatty Coon opened his eyes he expected to see Johnnie Green all ready to seize him. But to his great surprise he was still far above the ground. You see, Farmer Green had been mistaken. Either the big chestnut tree was taller than he had guessed, or the woods were nearer than he had thought. For instead of dropping upon the ground, Fatty's tree had fallen right against another tree on the edge of the woods. And there it lay, half-tipped over, with its branches caught fast in the branches of that other tree.

It was no wonder that Johnnie Green shouted. And he shouted still more loudly when he saw Fatty scramble out of the big chestnut and into the other tree, and out of that tree and into another, and then out of THAT tree. Fatty was going straight into the woods.

It was no wonder that Johnnie Green shouted. For he had lost his pet coon. He had lost him before he ever had him. And he was sadly disappointed.

But Fatty Coon was not disappointed, for he had not wanted to be a pet at all. And he was very glad—you may be sure—to get safely home once more.

X

FATTY COON AND THE MONSTER

One night Fatty Coon was strolling along the road that wound through the valley. He was in no hurry, for he had just left Farmer Green's apple orchard, where he had bolted all the apples he could possibly eat. The night was dark and though it was not very late, all the country people seemed to be in bed. There were no farmers driving along the road. Fatty had it all to himself. And so he walked slowly homewards. It was then that the terrible monster almost caught him.

This is how it all happened. There was a br-br-br-r-r-r in the air. Fatty really should have heard it long before he did. But he had eaten so many apples that he had begun to feel sleepy; and his ears were not so sharp as they should have been. And when at last Fatty heard that br-r-r-r it was quite loud. He was startled. And he stopped right in the middle of the road to listen. Fatty had never heard such a sound before.

The strange animal was on him before he knew it. Its glaring eyes blinded him. And if it had not screamed at him Fatty would never have escaped. It was the terrible screech of the monster which finally made Fatty jump. It was a frightful cry — like six wildcats all wailing together. And Fatty leaped to one side of the road just before the monster reached him.

The great creature went past Fatty like the wind and tore on up the hill. He seemed to be running so fast that he could not stop. Fatty could hear him panting as he climbed the sharp rise of the road.

Fatty Coon hurried away. He wanted to get home before the monster could stop and come back to look for him.

When Fatty told his mother about his narrow escape Mrs. Coon became much excited. She felt sure that Fatty was not mistaken, for had she not heard that strange cry herself?

There it was again! Woo-ooo-ooo-oo-o! It began low, rose to a shriek, and then died away again.

Mrs. Coon and Fatty climbed to the very top of their old poplar and gazed down the valley.

"Look, Mother!" Fatty cried. "He's stopped at Farmer Green's! You can see his eyes from here!"

Mrs. Coon looked. Sure enough! It was just as Fatty said. And that horrid call echoed across the valley once more.

Farmer Green stuck his head out of his chamber-window, to see what the man in the automobile wanted.

"Where's the nearest village, please?" the stranger asked. And after

Farmer Green had told him the man drove his car on again.

From their tree-top Fatty and his mother watched the monster dash down the valley. They knew he had gone, because they could see the gleam of those awful eyes.

"Do you suppose he ate up Farmer Green and his family?" Fatty asked in a frightened voice.

"I hope so," she said. "Then perhaps there'll be no more traps in the woods."

"But who would plant the corn?" Fatty asked.

Mrs. Coon did not appear to hear his question.

JASPER JAY TELLS SOME NEWS

It was quite late in the fall, and the weather had grown very cold. Mrs. Coon and her family had not left their home for several days; but on this day she thought it would be pleasant to go out in the sunshine and get a breath of fresh air and a bite to eat.

Fatty was the only one of her children that was not asleep; and he complained of being very hungry. So Mrs. Coon decided to take him with her.

The hunting was not very good. There were no birds' eggs at all to be found in the trees. The river and the brook and the creek were all frozen over, so Fatty and his mother could not catch any fish. And as for corn— Farmer Green had long ago gathered the last ear of it. Fatty wished that it was summertime. But it only made him hungrier than ever, to think of all the good things to eat that summer brings. He was feeling very unhappy when his mother said to him sharply —

"Run up this tree! Hurry, now! Don't ask any questions."

Now, Fatty did not always mind his mother as quickly as he might have. But this time he saw that she had stopped and was sniffing the air as if there was something about it she did not like.

That was enough for Fatty. He scrambled up the nearest tree. For he knew that his mother had discovered danger of some sort.

Mrs. Coon followed close behind Fatty. And they had no sooner hidden in the branches than Fatty saw what it was that his mother had smelled.

It was Johnnie Green! He passed right underneath the tree where they were perched. And as Mrs. Coon peeped down at him she shuddered and shivered and shook so hard that Fatty couldn't help noticing it.

"What's the matter?" he asked, as soon as Johnnie Green was out of sight.

"His cap!" Mrs. Coon exclaimed. "He is wearing a coon-skin cap!" Now do you wonder that she was upset? "Don't ever go near Farmer Green's house," she warned Fatty. "You don't want to be made into a cap, or a pair of gloves, or a coat, or anything like that, do you?"

"No, indeed, Mother!" Fatty was quite sure that such an adventure wouldn't please him at all. And he told himself right then and there that he would never go anywhere near Farmer Green's house. We shall see how well Fatty remembered.

That very afternoon Fatty Coon heard some very pleasant news. It was

Jasper Jay who told him.

Jasper Jay was a very noisy blue jay who lived in the neighborhood. He did not go south with most of the other birds when the cold weather came. He liked the winter and he was forever tearing about the woods, squalling and scolding at everybody. He was a very noisy fellow.

Well! when Fatty and his mother had reached home after their hunt, Fatty stayed out of doors. He climbed to the top of a tall pine tree nearby and stretched himself along a limb, to enjoy the sunshine, which felt very good upon his broad back. It was there that Jasper Jay found him and told him the pleasant news. And Fatty was very glad to hear the news, because he was still hungry.

This is what Jasper Jay told Fatty: he told him that Farmer Green had as many as forty fat turkeys, which roosted every night in a spreading oak in Farmer Green's front yard.

"If I liked turkeys I would certainly go down there some night and get one," said Jasper Jay.

FORTY FAT TURKEYS

When Jasper Jay told Fatty Coon about Farmer Green's forty fat turkeys Fatty felt hungrier than ever.

"Oh! I mustn't go near Farmer Green's house!" he said. "My mother told me to keep away from there. . . . What time did you say the turkeys go to roost?"

"Oh! they go to roost every night at sundown," Jasper Jay explained. "And there they sit, up in the tree, all night long. They're fast asleep. And you would have no trouble at all in catching as many as you wanted. . . . But of course, if you're afraid — why there's no use of MY talking about it. There's a plenty of other coons in these woods who'd be glad to know about those turkeys. And maybe they'd have the manners to say 'Thank you!' too." And with a hoarse, sneering laugh Jasper Jay flew away.

That was enough for Fatty. He made up his mind that he would show Jasper Jay that HE was not afraid. And he wanted a turkey to eat, too. He said nothing to his mother about Jasper's news. But that very night, when the moon came up, and the lights in Farmer Green's house were all out, Fatty Coon went stealing across the fields.

He was not afraid, for he knew that Farmer Green and all his family were in their beds. And it was so cold that Fatty felt sure that Farmer Green's dogs would be inside their kennels.

Fatty did not intend to make any noise. The turkeys were asleep — so Jasper Jay had told him — and he expected to grab one of them so swiftly and silently that the other turkeys would never know it.

When Fatty Coon came to Farmer Green's yard he had no trouble at all in finding the spreading oak. He could see the turkeys plainly where they dozed on the bare branches. And in less time than it takes to tell it Fatty had climbed the tree. On the very lowest limb there was a row of four plump turkeys, all sound asleep. And Fatty reached out and seized the nearest one. He seized the turkey by the neck, so that the big bird could not call out. But Fatty was not quite quick enough. Before he could pull her off her perch the turkey began to flap her wings, and she struck the turkey next her, so that THAT turkey woke up and began to gobble and flap HER wings. Then the next turkey on the limb woke up. And the first thing that Fatty Coon knew, every one of the thirty-nine turkeys that were left was going gobble-gob-gob-gob-gobble! And some of them went sailing off across the yard. One of them lighted on top of the porch just outside Farmer Green's window and it seemed to Fatty that that one made the greatest racket of all.

Farmer Green's window flew up; and Farmer Green's voice called "Spot! Spot!"

Fatty Coon did not wait to hear anything more. He dropped the turkey he had seized and slipped down to the ground. And then he ran toward the woods as fast as he could go.

Farmer Green's dog Spot was barking now. And Fatty wanted to climb one of the trees by the roadside. But he remembered, the narrow escape he had had when the dog had treed him near the cornfield. So he never stopped until he reached the woods. Then he went nimbly up into the trees. And while Spot was barking at the foot of the first tree he climbed, Fatty was travelling through the tree-tops toward home.

He never said anything to his mother about Farmer Green's turkeys. But the next time he saw Jasper Jay Fatty told him exactly what he thought of him.

"Ha! ha!" Jasper Jay only laughed. And he did not seem at all surprised that Fatty had fallen into trouble. To tell the truth, he was only sorry because Fatty had escaped. Jasper Jay did not like Fatty Coon. And he had told him about the forty fat turkeys because he hoped that Fatty would get caught if he tried to steal one of them.

"Wait till I catch you!" Fatty said.

But Jasper Jay only laughed harder than ever when Fatty said that. He seemed to think it was a great joke. He was most annoying.

XIII

FATTY MEETS JIMMY RABBIT

For once Fatty Coon was not hungry. He had eaten so much of Farmer

Green's corn that he felt as if he could not swallow another mouthful.

He was strolling homewards through the woods when someone called to

him.

It was Jimmy Rabbit.

"Where are you going, Fatty?" Jimmy Rabbit asked.

"Home!" said Fatty.

"Are you hungry?" Jimmy Rabbit asked anxiously.

"I should say not!" Fatty answered. "I've just had the finest meal I ever ate

in my life."

Jimmy Rabbit seemed to be relieved to hear that.

"Come on over and play," he said. "My brother and I are playing barber-

shop over in the old sycamore tree; and we need you."

"All right!" said Fatty. It was not often that any of the smaller forest-people

were willing to play with him, because generally Fatty couldn't help

getting hungry and then he usually tried to eat his playmates. "What do

you need me for?" Fatty asked, as he trudged along beside Jimmy Rabbit.

"We need you for the barber's pole," Jimmy explained. "You can come

inside the hollow tree and stick your tail out through a hole. It will make a

fine barber's pole — though the stripes DO run the wrong way, to be sure."

Fatty Coon was greatly pleased. He looked around at his tail and felt very

proud.

"I've got a beautiful tail — haven't I?" he asked.

"Um—yes!" Jimmy Rabbit replied, "though I must say it isn't one that I would care for myself... But come along! There may be people waiting to get their hair cut."

Sure enough! When they reached the make-believe barber-shop there was a gray squirrel inside, and Jimmy Rabbit's brother was busily snipping the fur off Mr. Squirrel's head.

"How much do you charge for a hair-cut?" Fatty asked.

"Oh, that depends!" Jimmy Rabbit said. "Mr. Squirrel will pay us six cabbage leaves. But if we were to cut your hair we'd have to ask more. We'd want a dozen cabbage leaves, at least."

"Well, don't I get anything for the use of my tail?" Fatty asked. He had already stuck it out through the hole; and he had half a mind to pull it in again.

Jimmy Rabbit and his brother whispered together for a few moments.

"I'll tell you what we'll do," Jimmy said. "If you'll let us use your tail for the barber's pole, we'll cut your hair free. Isn't that fair enough?"

Fatty Coon was satisfied. But he insisted that Jimmy begin to cut his hair at once.

"I'm doing my part of the work now," he pointed out. "So there's no reason why you shouldn't do yours."

With that Jimmy Rabbit began. He clipped and snipped at Fatty's head, pausing now and then to see the effect. He smiled once in a while, behind Fatty's back, because Fatty certainly did look funny with his fur all ragged and uneven.

"Moustache trimmed?" Jimmy Rabbit asked, when he had finished with

Fatty's head.

"Certainly—of course!" Fatty Coon answered. And pretty soon Fatty's long white moustache lay on the floor of the barber-shop. Fatty felt a bit uneasy as he looked down and saw his beautiful moustache lying at his feet. "You haven't cut it too short, I hope," he said.

"No, indeed!" Jimmy Rabbit assured him. "It's the very latest style."

"What on earth has happened to you?" Mrs. Coon cried,—when Fatty reached home that night. "Have you been in a fire?"

"It's the latest style, Mother," Fatty told her. "At least, that's what

Jimmy Rabbit says." He felt the least bit uneasy again.

"Did you let that Jimmy Rabbit do that to you?" Mrs. Coon asked.

Fatty hung his head. He said nothing at all. But his mother knew.

"Well! you ARE a sight!" she exclaimed. "It will be months before you look like my child again. I shall be ashamed to go anywhere with you."

Fatty Coon felt very foolish. And there was just one thing that kept him from crying. And THAT was THIS: he made up his mind that when he played barber-shop with Jimmy Rabbit again he would get even with him.

But when the next day came, Fatty couldn't find Jimmy Rabbit and his brother anywhere. They kept out of sight. But they had told all the other forest-people about the trick they had played on Fatty Coon. And everywhere Fatty went he heard nothing but hoots and jeers and laughs. He felt very silly. And he wished that he might meet Jimmy Rabbit and his brother.

XIV

THE BARBER-SHOP AGAIN

Although Fatty Coon never could get Jimmy Rabbit and his brother to play barber-shop with him again, Fatty saw no reason why he should not play the game without them. So one day he led his brother Blackie over to the old hollow sycamore. His sisters, Fluffy and Cutey, wanted to go too. But Fatty would not let them. "Girls can't be barbers," he said. And of course they could find no answer to that.

As soon as Fatty and Blackie reached the old sycamore I am sorry to say that a dispute arose. Each of them wanted to use his own tail for the barber's pole. They couldn't both stick their tails through the hole in the tree at the same time. So they finally agreed to take turns.

Playing barber-shop wasn't so much fun as they had expected, because nobody would come near to get his hair cut. You see, the smaller forest-people were all afraid to go inside that old sycamore where Fatty and Blackie were. There was no telling when the two brothers might get so hungry they would seize and eat a rabbit or a squirrel or a chipmunk. And you know it isn't wise to run any such risk as that.

Fatty offered to cut Blackie's hair. But Blackie remembered what his mother had said when Fatty came home with his moustache gone and his head all rough and uneven. So Blackie wouldn't let Fatty touch him. But HE offered to cut Fatty's hair — what there was left of it.

"No, thank you!" said Fatty. "I only get my hair cut once a month." Of course, he had never had his hair cut except that once, in his whole life.

Now, since there was so little to do inside the hollow tree, Fatty and Blackie kept quarreling. Blackie would no sooner stick his tail through the hole in the side of the tree than Fatty would want HIS turn. And when Fatty had succeeded in squeezing HIS tail out through the opening Blackie would insist that Fatty's time was up.

It was Fatty's turn, and Blackie was shouting to him to stand aside and give him a chance.

"I won't!" said Fatty. "I'm going to stay here just as long as I please."

The words were hardly out of his mouth when he gave a sharp squeal, as if something hurt him. And he tried to pull his tail out of the hole. He wanted to get it out now. But alas! it would not come! It was caught fast! And the harder Fatty pulled the more it hurt him.

"Go out and see what's the matter!" he cried to Blackie.

But Blackie wouldn't stir. He was afraid to leave the shelter of the hollow tree.

"It may be a bear that has hold of your tail," he told Fatty. And somehow, that idea made Fatty tremble all over.

"Oh, dear! oh, dear!" he wailed. "What shall I do? Oh! whatever shall I do?" He began to cry. And Blackie cried too. How Fatty wished that his mother was there to tell him what to do!

But he knew of no way to fetch her. Even if she were at home she could never hear him calling from inside the tree. So Fatty gave up all hope of her helping.

"Please, Mr. Bear, let go of my tail!" he cried, when he could stand the pain no longer.

The only answer that came was a low growl, which frightened Fatty and Blackie more than ever. And then, just as they both began to howl at the top of their voices Fatty's tail was suddenly freed. He was pulling on it so hard that he fell all in a heap on the floor of the barber-shop. And that surprised him.

But he was still more surprised when he heard his mother say—

"Stop crying and come out—both of you!" Fatty and Blackie scrambled out of the hollow sycamore. Fatty looked all around. But there was no bear to be seen anywhere—no one but his mother.

"Did you frighten the bear away, Mother?" he asked.

"There was no bear," Mrs. Coon told him. "And it's lucky for you that there wasn't. I saw your tail sticking out of this tree and I thought I would teach you a lesson. Now, don't ever do such a foolish thing again. Just think what a fix you would have been in if Johnnie Green had come along. He could have caught you just as easily as anything."

Fatty Coon was so glad to be free once more that he promised to be good forever after. And he was just as good as any little coon could be — all the rest of that day.

FATTY VISITS THE SMOKE-HOUSE

The winter was fast going. And one fine day in February Fatty Coon crept out of his mother's house to enjoy the warm sunshine—and see what he could find to eat.

Fatty was much thinner than he had been in the fall. He had spent so much of the time sleeping that he had really eaten very little. And now he hardly knew himself as he looked at his sides. They no longer stuck out as they had once.

After nosing about the swamp and the woods all the afternoon Fatty decided that there was no use in trying to get a meal there. The ground was covered with snow. And except for rabbit tracks—and a few squirrels'—he could find nothing that even suggested food. And looking at those tracks only made him hungrier than ever.

For a few minutes Fatty thought deeply. And then he turned about and went straight toward Farmer Green's place. He waited behind the fence just beyond Farmer Green's house; and when it began to grow dark he crept across the barnyard.

As Fatty passed a small, low building he noticed a delicious smell. And he stopped right there. He had gone far enough. The door was open a little way. And after one quick look all around—to make sure there was nobody to see him—Fatty slipped inside.

It was almost dark inside Farmer Green's smokehouse—for that was what the small, low building was called. It was almost dark; but Fatty could see just as well as you and I can see in the daytime. There was a long row of hams hung up in a line. Underneath them were white ashes, where Farmer Green had built wood fires, to smoke the hams. But the fires were out, now; and Fatty was in no danger of being burned.

The hams were what Fatty Coon had smelled. And the hams were what Fatty intended to eat. He decided that he would eat them all—though of course he could never have done that—at least, not in one night; nor in a week, either. But when it came to eating, Fatty's courage never failed him. He would have tried to eat an elephant, if he had had the chance.

Fatty did not stop to look long at that row of hams. He climbed a post that ran up the side of the house and he crept out along the pole from which the hams were hung.

He stopped at the very first ham he came to. There was no sense in going any further. And Fatty dropped on top of the ham and in a twinkling he had torn off a big, delicious mouthful.

Fatty could not eat fast enough. He wished he had two mouths—he was so hungry. But he did very well, with only ONE. In no time at all he had made a great hole in the ham. And he had no idea of stopping. But he did stop. He stopped very suddenly. For the first thing he knew, something threw him right down upon the floor. And the ham fell on top of him and nearly knocked him senseless.

He choked and spluttered; for the ashes filled his mouth and his eyes, and his ears, too. For a moment he lay there on his back; but soon he managed to kick the heavy ham off his stomach and then he felt a little better. But he was terribly frightened. And though his eyes smarted so he could hardly see, he sprang up and found the doorway.

Fatty swallowed a whole mouthful of ashes as he dashed across the barnyard. And he never stopped running until he was almost home. He was puzzled. Try as he would, he couldn't decide what it was that had flung him upon the floor. And when he told his mother about his adventure—as he did a whole month later—she didn't know exactly what had happened, either.

"It was some sort of trap, probably," Mrs. Coon said.

But for once Mrs. Coon was mistaken.

It was very simple. In his greedy haste Fatty had merely bitten through the cord that fastened the ham to the pole. And of course it had at once fallen, carrying Fatty with it!

But what do you suppose? Afterward, when Fatty had grown up, and had children of his own, he often told them about the time he had escaped from the trap in Farmer Green's smokehouse.

Fatty's children thought it very exciting. It was their favorite story.

And they made their father tell it over and over again.

FATTY COON PLAYS ROBBER

After Fatty Coon played barber-shop with Jimmy Rabbit and his brother it was a long time before he met them again. But one day Fatty was wandering through the woods when he caught sight of Jimmy. Jimmy dodged behind a tree. And Fatty saw Jimmy's brother peep from behind another. You see, his ears were so long that they stuck far beyond the tree, and Fatty couldn't help seeing them.

"Hello!" Fatty called. "I'm glad to see you." And he told the truth, too. He had been trying to find those two brothers for weeks, because he wanted to get even with them for cutting off his moustache. Jimmy and his brother hopped out from behind their trees.

"Hello!" said Jimmy. "We were just looking for you." Probably he meant to say, "We were just looking AT you." He was somewhat upset by meeting Fatty; for he knew that Fatty was angry with him.

"Oh, ho! You were, were you?" Fatty answered. He began to slide down the tree he had been climbing.

Jimmy Rabbit and his brother edged a little further away.

"Better not come too near us!" he said. "We've both got the pink-eye, and you don't want to catch it."

Fatty paused and looked at the brothers. Sure enough! their eyes were as pink as anything.

"Does it hurt much?" Fatty asked.

"Well—it does and it doesn't," Jimmy replied. "I just stuck a brier into one of my eyes a few minutes ago and it hurt awful, then. But you'll be perfectly safe, so long as you don't touch us."

"How long does it last?" Fatty inquired.

"Probably we'll never get over it," Jimmy Rabbit said cheerfully. And his brother nodded his head, as much as to say, "That's so!"

Fatty Coon was just the least bit alarmed. He really thought that there was something the matter with their eyes. You see, though the Rabbit brothers' eyes were always pink (for they were born that way), he had never noticed it before. So Fatty thought it would be safer not to go too near them.

"Well, it's too bad," he told Jimmy. "I'm sorry. I wanted to play with you."

"Oh, that's all right!" Jimmy said. "We can play, just the same. I'll tell you what we'll play. We'll play—"

"Not barber-shop!" Fatty interrupted. "I won't play barber-shop, I never liked that game."

Jimmy Rabbit started to smile. But he turned his smile into a sneeze.

And he said—

"We'll play robber. You'll like that, I know. And you can be the robber.

You look like one, anyhow."

That remark made Fatty Coon angry. And he wished that Jimmy hadn't the pink-eye. He would have liked to make an end of him right then and there.

"What do you mean?" he shouted. "Robber nothing! I'm just as good as you are!"

"Of course, of course!" Jimmy said hastily. "It's your face, you know, That black patch covers your eyes just like a robber's mask. That's why we want you to be the robber."

Fatty had slipped down his tree to the ground; and now he looked down into the creek. It was just as Jimmy said. Fatty had never thought of it before, but the black patch of short fur across the upper part of his face made him look exactly like a robber.

"Come on!" said Jimmy. "We can't play the game without you."

"Well—all right!" said Fatty. He began to feel proud of his mask. "What shall I do?"

"You wait right here," Jimmy ordered. "Hide behind that tree. We'll go into the woods. And when we come back past this spot you jump out and say 'Hands up!' ... You understand?"

"Of course!" said Fatty. "But hurry up! Don't be gone long."

"Leave that to us," said Jimmy Rabbit. He winked at his brother; and they started off together.

Fatty Coon did not see that wink. If he had, he wouldn't have waited there all the afternoon for those Rabbit brothers to return. They never came back at all. And they told everybody about the trick they had played on Fatty Coon. For a long time after that wherever Fatty went the forest-people called "Robber!" after him. And Jasper Jay was the most annoying of all, because whenever he shouted "Robber!" he always laughed so loudly and so long. His hoarse screech echoed through the woods. And the worst of it was, everybody knew what he was laughing at.

FATTY FINDS THE MOON

Wandering through the woods one day, Fatty Coon's bright eyes caught a strange gleam from something—something that shone and glittered out of the green. Fatty wanted to see what it was, though he hardly thought it was anything to eat. But whenever he came upon something new he always wanted to examine it. So now Fatty hurried to see what the strange thing was.

It was the oddest thing he had ever found—flat, round, and silvery; and it hung in the air, under a tree, just over Fatty's head. Fatty Coon looked carefully at the bright thing. He walked all around it, so he could see it from all sides. And at last he thought he knew what it was. He made up his mind that it was the moon!

He had often seen the moon up in the sky; and here it was, just the same size exactly, hanging so low that he could have reached it with his paw. He saw nothing strange in that; for he knew that the moon often touched the earth. Had he not seen it many a time, resting on the side of Blue Mountain? One night he had asked his mother if he might go up on the mountain to play with the moon; but she had only laughed. And here, at last, was the moon come to him! Fatty was so excited that he ran home as fast as he could go, to tell his mother, and his brother Blackie, and Fluffy and Cutey, his sisters.

"Oh! the moon! the moon!" Fatty shouted. He had run so fast that, being so plump, he was quite out of breath. And that was all he could say.

"Well, well! What about the moon!" Mrs. Coon asked. "Anybody would think you had found it, almost." And she smiled.

Fatty puffed and gasped. And at last he caught his breath again.

"Yes—I've found it! It's over in the woods—just a little way from here!" he said. "Big, and round, and shiny! Let's all go and bring it home!"

"Well, well, well!" Mrs. Coon was puzzled. She had never heard of the moon being found in those woods; and she hardly knew what to think. "Are you sure?" she asked.

"Oh, yes, Mother!" Fatty could hardly wait, he was so eager to lead the way. And with many a shake of the head, Mrs. Coon, with her family, started off to see the moon.

"There!" Fatty cried, as they came in sight of the bright, round thing.

"There it is—just as I told you!" And they all set up a great shouting.

All but Mrs. Coon. She wasn't quite sure, even yet, that Fatty had really found the moon. And she walked close to the shining thing and peered at it. But not too close! Mrs. Coon didn't go too near it. And she told her children quite sternly to stand back. It was well that she did; for when Mrs. Coon took her eyes off Fatty's moon and looked at the ground beneath it— well! she jumped back so quickly that she knocked two of her children flat on the ground.

A trap! THAT was what Mrs. Coon saw right in front of her. And Farmer Green, or his boy, or whoever it was that set the trap, had hung that bright piece of TIN over the trap hoping that one of her family would see it and play with it—and fall into the trap. Yes—it was a mercy that Fatty hadn't begun knocking it about. For if he had he would have stepped right into the trap and it would have shut—SNAP! Just like that. And there he would have been, caught fast.

It was no wonder that Mrs. Coon hurried her family away from that spot. And Fatty led them all home again. He couldn't get away from his moon fast enough.

THE LOGGERS COME

Fatty Coon was frightened; he had just waked up and he heard a sound that was exactly like the noise Farmer Green and his hired man had made when they cut down the tall chestnut tree where he was perched.

"Oh, Mother! What is it?" he cried.

"The loggers have come," Mrs. Coon said. "They are cutting down all the big trees in the swamp."

"Then we'll have to move, won't we?" Fatty asked.

"No! They won't touch this tree," his mother told him. "It's an old tree, and hollow—so they won't chop it down. It's only the good sound trees that they'll take."

"But I thought this was a good tree." Fatty was puzzled.

"So it is, my son! It's a good tree for us. But not for the loggers.

They would have little use for it."

Fatty Coon felt better when he heard that. And he had a good deal of fun, peeping down at the loggers and watching them work. But he took care that they should not see HIM. He knew what their bright axes could do.

When night came Fatty had still more fun. When the loggers were asleep Fatty went to their camp in the woods beside the brook and he found many good things to eat. He did not know the names of all the goodies; but he ate them just the same. He 'specially liked some potatoes which the careless cook had left in a pan near the open camp-fire. The fire was out. And the pan rested on a stump close beside it. Fatty Coon climbed up and crawled right inside the pan. And after he had had one taste of those potatoes he grew so excited—they were so good—that he tipped the pan off the stump and the potatoes rolled right into the ashes.

Fatty had jumped to one side, when the tin pan fell. It made a great clatter; and he kept very still for a few moments, while he listened. But no one stirred. And then Fatty jumped plump into the ashes.

WHEW! He jumped out again as fast as he could; for beneath the ashes there were plenty of hot coals. Fatty stood in them for not more than three seconds, but that was quite long enough. The bottoms of his feet burned as if a hundred hornets had stung them.

He stood first on one foot and then on another. If you could have seen him you would have thought Fatty was dancing. And you might have laughed, because he looked funny.

But Fatty Coon did not laugh. In fact, he came very near crying. And he did not wait to eat another mouthful. He limped along toward home. And it was several days before he stirred out of his mother's house again. He just lay in his bed and waited until his burns were well again.

It was very hard. For Fatty did not like to think of all those good things to eat that he was missing. And he hoped the loggers would not go away before his feet were well again.

XIX

FATTY GROWS EVEN FATTER

When Fatty Coon's burned feet were well once more, the very first night he left his mother's house he went straight to the loggers' camp. He did not wait long after dark, because he was afraid that some of his neighbors might have found that there were good things to eat about the camp. And Fatty wanted them all.

To his delight, there were goodies almost without end. He nosed about, picking up potato peelings, and bits of bacon. And perhaps the best of all was a piece of cornbread, which Fatty fairly gobbled. And then he found a box half-full of something—scraps that tasted like apples, only they were not round like apples, and they were quite dry, instead of being juicy. But Fatty liked them; and he ate them all, down to the smallest bit.

He was thirsty, then. So he went down to the brook, which ran close by the camp. The loggers had cut a hole through the ice, so they could get water. And Fatty crept close to the edge of the hole and drank. He drank a great deal of water, because he was very thirsty. And when he had finished he sat down on the ice for a time. He did not care to stir about just then. And he did not think he would ever want anything to eat again.

At last Fatty Coon rose to his feet. He felt very queer. There was a strange, tight feeling about his stomach. And his sides were no longer thin. They stuck out just as they had before winter came—only more so. And what alarmed Fatty was this: his sides seemed to be sticking out more and more all the time.

He wondered what he had been eating. Those dry things that tasted like apples—he wondered what they were.

Now, there was some printing on the outside of the box which held those queer, spongy, flat things. Of course, Fatty Coon could not read, so the printing did him no good at all. But if you had seen the box, and if you are old enough to read, you would have known that the printing said:

EVAPORATED APPLES

Now, evaporated apples are nothing more or less than dried apples. The cook of the loggers' camp used them to make apple pies. And first, before making his pies, he always soaked them in water so they would swell.

Now you see what made Fatty Coon feel so queer and uncomfortable. He had first eaten his dried apples. And then he had soaked them, by drinking out of the brook. It was no wonder that his sides stuck out, for the apples that he had bolted were swelling and puffing him out until he felt that he should burst. In fact, the wonder of it was that he was able to get through his mother's doorway, when he reached home.

But he did it, though it cost him a few groans. And he frightened his mother, too.

"I only hope you're not poisoned," she said, when Fatty told her what he had been doing.

And that remark frightened Fatty more than ever. He was sure he was never going to feel any better.

Poor Mrs. Coon was much worried all the rest of the night. But when morning came she knew that Fatty was out of danger. She knew it because of something he said. It was this:

"Oh, dear! I wish I had something to eat!"

THE TRACKS IN THE SNOW

One fine winter's day Fatty Coon came upon the queerest tracks in the snow. They were huge—a great deal bigger, even, than bear-tracks, which Fatty had sometimes seen, for once in a while, before the weather grew too cold, and he fell into his winter's sleep, a bear would come down into the valley from his home on Blue Mountain.

But these were six times as big as bear tracks. And Fatty felt a shiver of fear run up and down his back.

He followed the trail a little way. But he was very careful. He was always ready to scramble up a tree, in case he should suddenly see the strange animal—or rather, in case the strange animal should see HIM.

The great tracks led straight toward Farmer Green's house. And Fatty did not want to go there. So he hurried home to ask his mother what he had found. Mrs. Coon listened to Fatty's story.

"I think it must be the monster that almost caught me in the road last summer," said Fatty, meaning the automobile that had given him a great fright. "Maybe he's come back again to catch Farmer Green and his family … Do you suppose he's eaten them up?"

Mrs. Coon was puzzled. And she was somewhat alarmed, too. She wanted to see those strange tracks herself. So she told her other children not to step a foot out of the house until she came back. And then she asked Fatty to run along and show her where he had come upon the monster's trail.

Fatty Coon felt very important, as he led the way across the swamp and into the woods. It was not often that he could show his mother anything. And he was so proud that he almost forgot his fright.

"I guess you're glad I have sharp eyes," he said, as they hurried along.

"If the tracks are as big as you say they are, your eyes wouldn't have to be very sharp to see them," his mother told him. Mrs. Coon never liked to hear her children boast. She knew that boasting is one of the most unpleasant things anyone can do.

"Well—maybe you don't think I saw the monster's tracks at all," said

Fatty. "Maybe you don't think I heard him screech—"

"When did you hear him screech?" Mrs. Coon asked. "This is the first you've said about SCREECHING. When was it?"

"Last summer," Fatty answered.

Mrs. Coon didn't smile. Perhaps she was too worried for that.

"It may not be the same monster," she said. "It may not be a monster at all."

But by this time Fatty was sure he was right. He was sure he knew more than his mother.

"Why can't we go right over to Farmer Green's and take some of his chickens?" he asked. "The monster has probably eaten him by this time, and all his family, too."

But Mrs. Coon would do no such thing.

"Show me the tracks," she said firmly. And so they went on into the woods.

"There they are!" Fatty cried, a few minutes later. "See, Mother! They're even bigger than I said." He heard a funny noise behind him, then. And when Fatty Coon looked around he saw that his mother was actually holding her sides, she was laughing so hard.

"Those are Farmer Green's tracks," she said, as soon as she could stop laughing long enough to speak.

"What—as big as that?" Fatty pointed at the huge prints in the snow.

"Snowshoes!" Mrs. Coon said. "He was wearing snowshoes—great frames made of thongs and sticks, to keep him from sinking into the snow."

So that was all there was to Fatty's monster. Somehow, he was disappointed. But he was very glad he had said nothing to Jasper Jay about his strange animal. For if he had, he knew he would never have heard the last of it.

And Fatty was glad about another thing, too. He felt very happy that his mother had not let him go after Farmer Green's chickens.

THE END